Make a Snowman

written by Pam Holden
illustrated by Robin Van't Hof

We can make a good snowman.

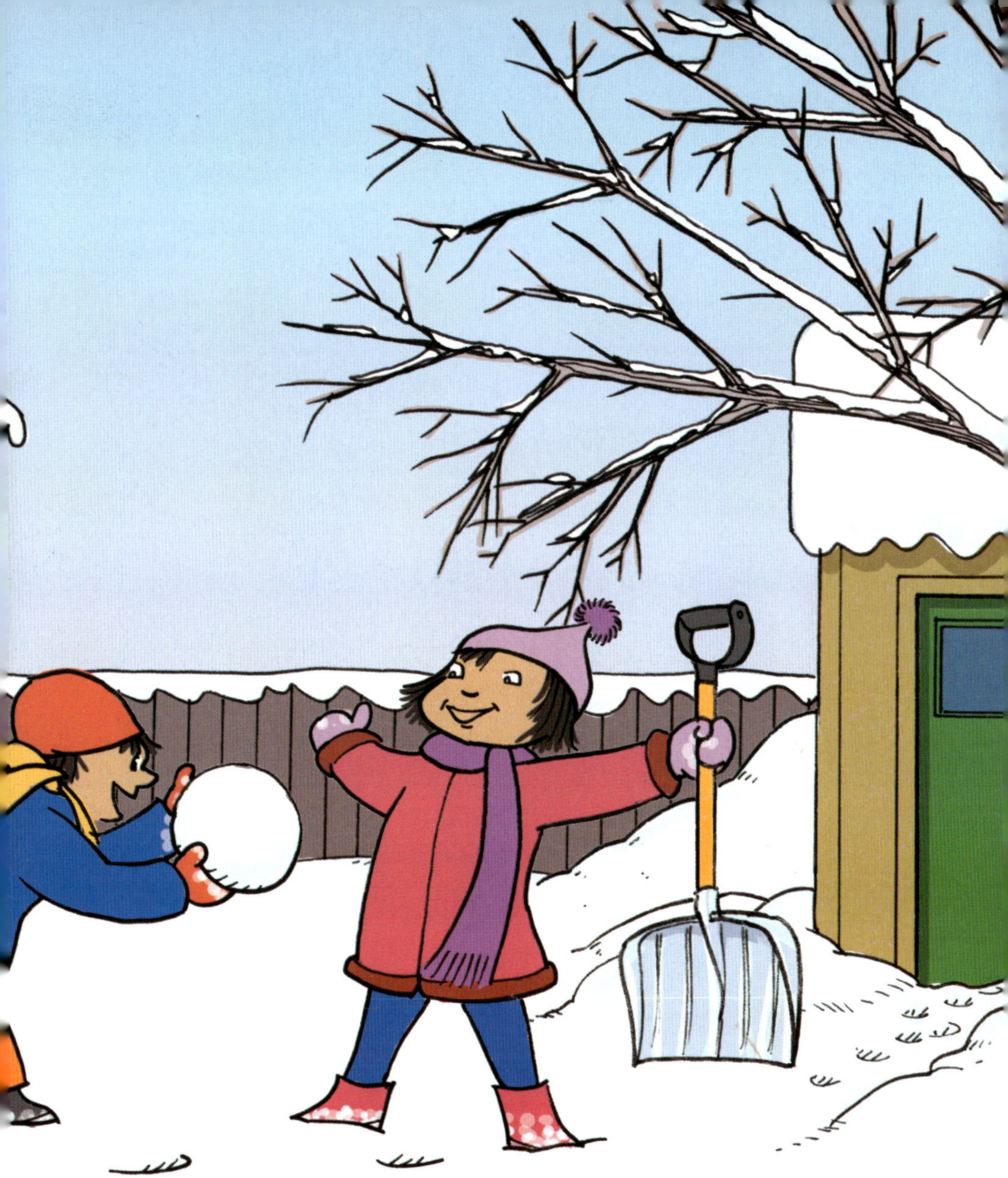

We make some
big balls of snow
like this.

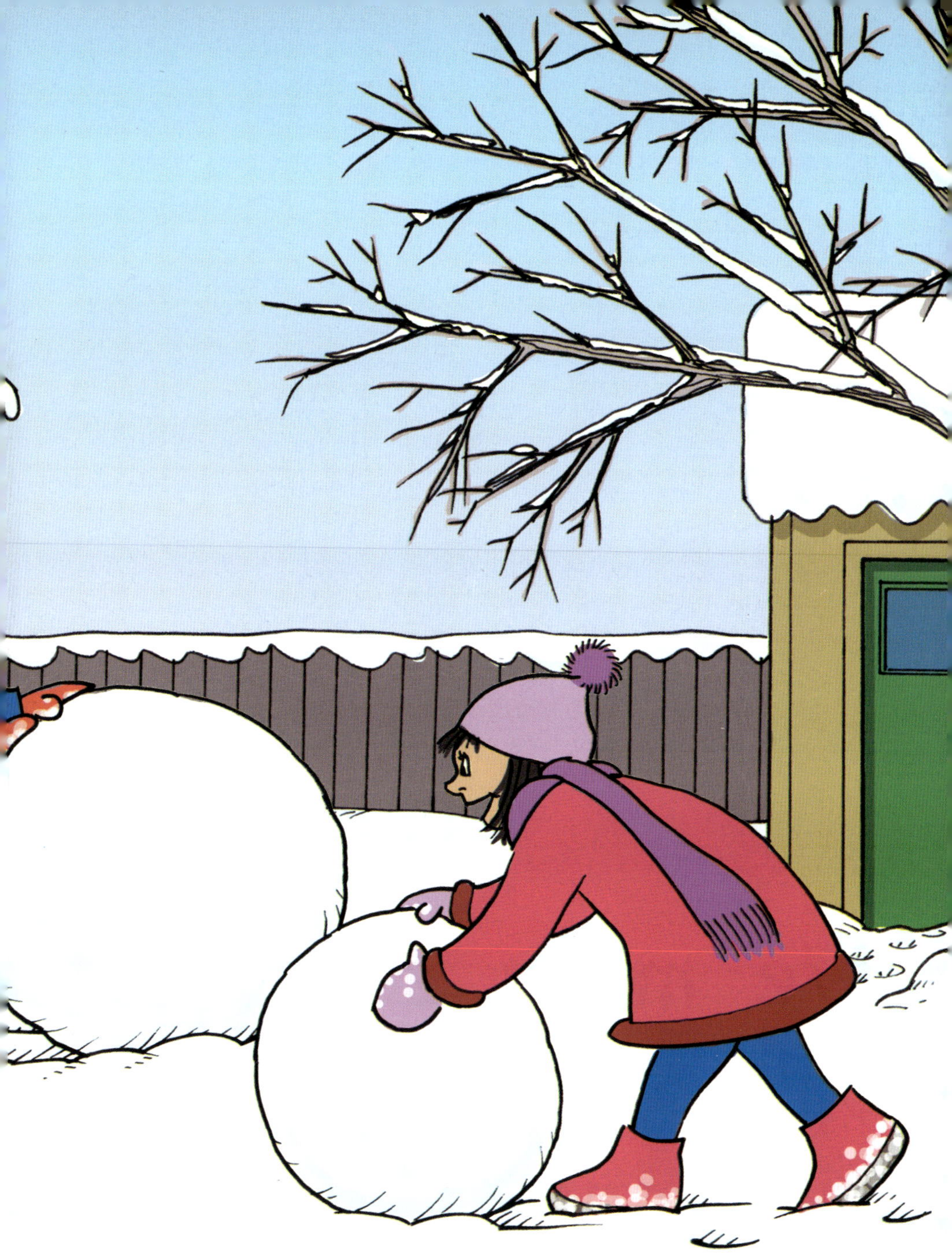

We make a little ball of snow for his head.

7

We put the little ball on the big balls like this.

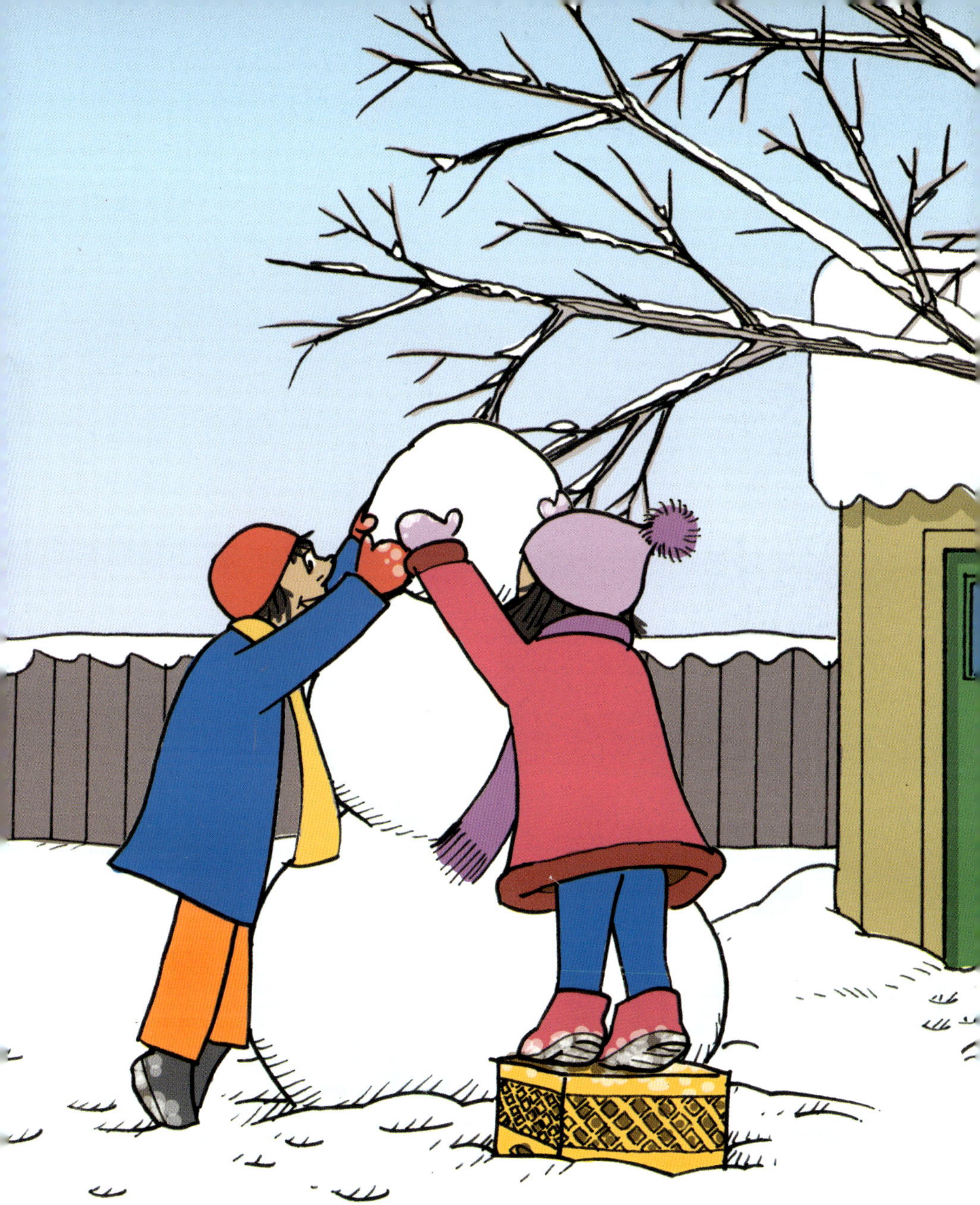

We put some sticks for his arms and a carrot for his nose.

11

We put some
buttons for his eyes
and some stones for
his mouth.

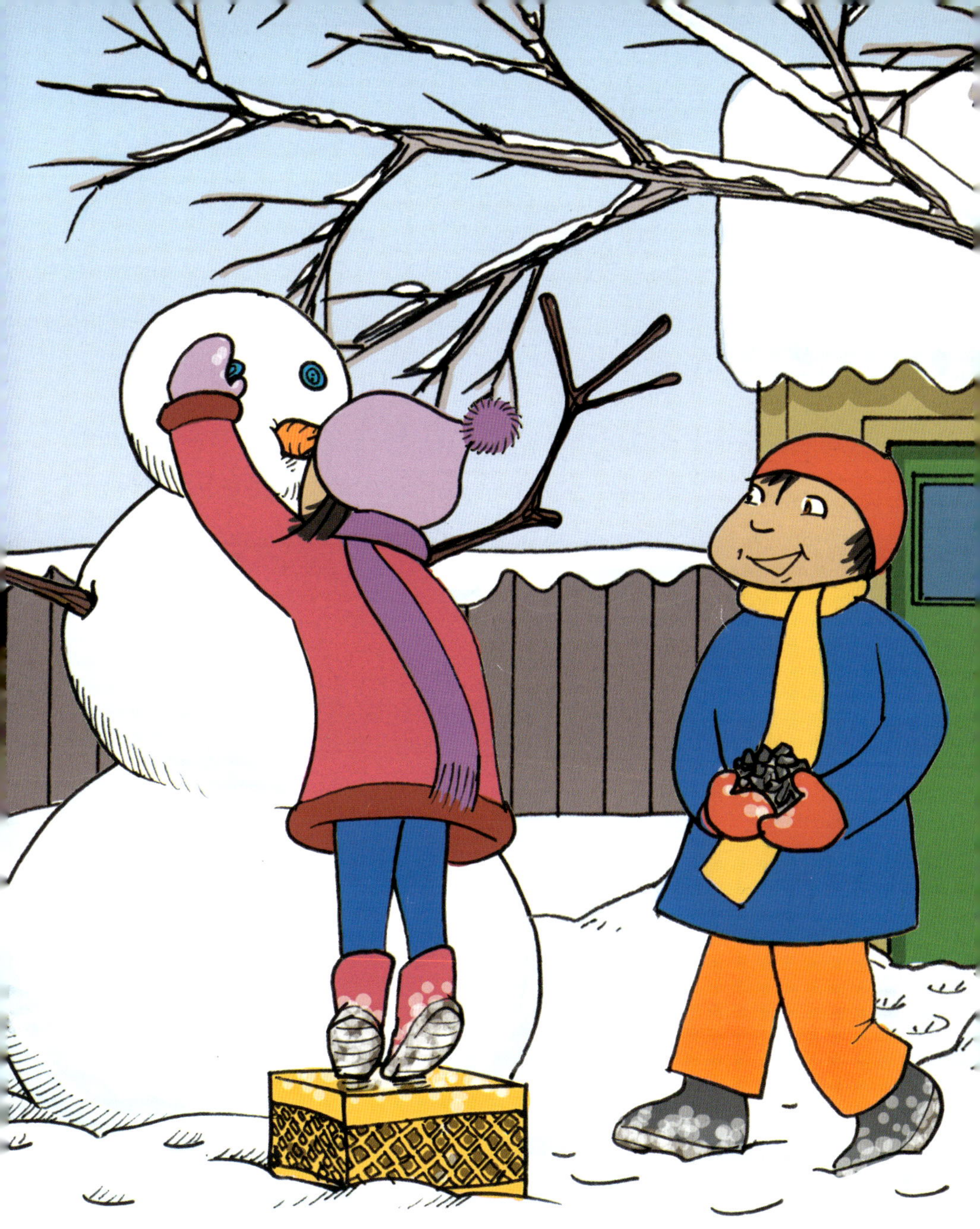

We put a hat on his head like this.

15

We have a
good snowman!